5/13

D1531016

Graveyard Diaries

HOW NOT TO BE KILLED BY A ZOMBIE

magic Wagon

by Baron Specter
illustrated by Setch Kneupper

visit us at www.abdopublishing.com

Printed in the United States of America, North Mankato, Minnesota.
052012
092012
 This book contains at least 10% recycled materials.

Text by Baron Specter
Illustrations by Setch Kneupper
Edited by Stephanie Hedlund and Rochelle Baltzer
Interior layout and design by Neil Klinepier
Cover design by Neil Klinepier

Library of Congress Cataloging-in-Publication Data

Specter, Baron, 1957-
  How not to be killed by a zombie / by Baron Specter ; illustrated by Setch Kneupper.
    p. cm. -- (Graveyard diaries ; bk. 3)
  Summary: Zombies are killing all the animals in Marshfield Grove Cemetery, and it is up to Barry Bannon and his friends to defeat the zombies and rescue the ghost dogs that they have trapped in a pit.
  ISBN 978-1-61641-900-4
  1. Ghost stories. 2. Zombies--Juvenile fiction. 3. Haunted cemeteries--Juvenile fiction. [1. Ghosts--Fiction. 2. Zombies--Fiction. 3. Haunted places--Fiction. 4. Cemeteries--Fiction.] I. Kneupper, Setch, ill. II. Title.
  PZ7.S741314How 2012
  813.6--dc23
                        2011052035

CONTENTS

WoodLand Cemetery
Jared's House
Marshfield Grove
Barry's House
MARSHFIELD

Chapter 1:
Lucy Got a Scare

Barry's Diary: Saturday, March 19. 7:05 p.m.

Lucy was scared in the cemetery. She usually pulls so hard on her leash that I can barely keep up. After dinner we were out near the old Marshfield Grove chapel. Lucy is always smelling for rabbits or squirrels. She had her head down and was following a trail, sniffing like crazy. Then she stopped. She started shaking and hid behind me.

I didn't see anything strange. But she kept staring at a gravestone. It said *Alma Simmons. Born 1850. Died 1862.* Twelve years old—just a year older than I am. I wonder if they had sixth grade back in the 1800s . . .

We walked home. Lucy kept looking back and

whining. Did she see a ghost? There are lots of them in our town. All four cemeteries are haunted. Lucy never seemed to be bothered by ghosts before. But now she's curled up on the floor of my bedroom. Her eyes are wide open. She's shivering.

Lucy got a scare

At Marshfield Chapel.

I don't know what was there.

Maybe a rotten apple.

I'm the king of stupid poems like that. It's my best talent. I'll go back to the cemetery tonight. I'll check Alma's grave again. Dogs can see things in daylight that we can't. But sometimes they're visible at night for humans.

Barry Bannon pulled open a drawer. He pushed aside some socks. He felt under his T-shirts. Where was his flashlight?

"Have you seen it?" he asked Lucy.

Lucy stood up and wagged her tail. She stretched back, straightening her front legs. Then she yawned.

Barry found the flashlight in a second drawer. He checked it. The beam was getting weak, so he changed the batteries. He patted Lucy on the head.

"Are you over that scare now?" he asked. "I'm going back out. You relax."

Lucy followed him down the stairs. She was a mutt, mostly a mix of Labrador and hound. Her hair was the color of cream. There was a golden streak along her spine. It went all the way to the tip of her tail.

In the kitchen, Lucy went straight to her leash. She pointed at it with her nose and looked up at Barry. Then she whined.

"Didn't you just walk her?" asked Barry's mother.

"Less than an hour ago," Barry said.

"Looks like she wants to go again," his mom said.

"Fine with me," Barry said. "I was going out anyway."

When they got outside, Barry knelt next to Lucy. "I thought you were scared," he said. "I'm going back by the chapel. Are you sure you want to come?"

Lucy started pulling, heading for the cemetery. Barry followed.

Marshfield Grove was the biggest of the four cemeteries in town. The Bannons lived right by the entrance. Barry had friends who lived on the edges of each of the other graveyards. They often got together to talk about scary things they'd seen or heard. Several times they'd fought ghosts or other spirits. They called their group the Zombie Hunters.

Barry's friend Mitch lived next to Evergreen Cemetery. It was swampy and had thick bushes. Stan lived at the edge of Hilltop Cemetery. Amy lived near Stan. And Jared's house was next to Woodland Cemetery.

Because there were so many cemeteries,

the town of Marshfield was also known as "Graveyard City."

There was a stiff breeze this evening. It rattled the branches of the trees. No leaves were out yet. The trees were just beginning to show the first signs of new buds. There had been snow on the ground just a few days before. It had melted in a hurry on one warm day. Tonight it was cool again.

Lucy kept her head down, sniffing every inch of the trail. They walked this way at least twice every day. Each trip seemed new to Lucy. There was always a new smell. It was nearly spring, so the ground was thawing. That brought many old smells, too.

Barry thought he heard a girl's voice calling. It sounded like it called for Lucy.

Just the wind, he thought.

The trees were tall and thick. Even on a sunny day, these patches of woods were dark. At night, like this, you couldn't see far at all.

Lucy stopped and leaned toward a spot on the hill. She touched it with her nose.

"I guess a mouse crossed that spot, huh?" Barry said. "Or maybe a bird landed there."

Barry heard the girl's voice again. He was sure she said, "Lucy!"

Lucy kept sniffing and pulling. But when Barry turned toward the chapel, she stopped.

"It's okay," Barry said. "We won't get too close."

Lucy stayed right at his side as they climbed the hill. The simple chapel was square and made of stones. It had been empty for years. The door and windows were boarded up. The sun never shined on the chapel because of the very tall pine trees.

There were a few dozen graves in a shaded spot behind the chapel. All were from the 1800s. The gravestones were small and made of granite. The ground was bumpy.

The sky was fully dark now. Barry shined the flashlight on the stones. He held the beam on the one that said Alma Simmons.

Lucy let out a whimper. She was wagging her tail, but she looked scared.

Barry leaned over and rubbed her back.

"What do you see?" he whispered. "Who's there?"

Lucy took a step backward. She lowered her head and growled. She tucked her tail between her legs. Then she barked.

Barry stared at the gravestone. "Come on," he said, giving the leash a gentle tug. "Just a little closer."

Lucy dug in her feet. She wouldn't move. Barry stepped forward anyway, as far as the leash would let him.

He moved the light in a small circle. Everything seemed calm. The grass around the graves was brown. It was matted down from being under the snow all winter.

Barry took a few more steps. It was cold up here on the hill. He wished he'd worn gloves. A brisk wind hit him in the face. His teeth began to chatter.

"Guess we should go back," he said. He turned toward home.

But Lucy wasn't there!

"Lucy!" he called. He grabbed the end of the leash. The clasp was fine. But Lucy was nowhere to be seen.

How could she have gotten loose? She'd never run away. And he would have heard her run.

"Lucy!" he called again. His stomach felt tight and cold. She couldn't have gone far. But where was she?

He shined the light in a wide circle and called her name again. Lucy was his best friend. And she always stayed close by.

He ran partway down the hill, then back up. He looked behind a huge marble gravestone. Then he ran back toward the chapel, calling her name.

His heart sped up as he heard a familiar noise. It sounded like Lucy's dog tags shaking on her collar. Suddenly he saw her. She was running to him from behind the chapel.

Barry dropped to his knees and hugged

her tight. He clipped the leash to her collar. "How did you get loose?" he asked. "Why did you run?"

Lucy licked his face, then she pulled toward home. She was shaking again.

"Come on," Barry said, and they started running down the hill. As they reached the bottom, Barry heard the girl's voice calling from near the chapel.

"Lucy," she said, "where have you gone?"

Chills ran down Barry's spine.

Chapter 2:
Ghostly Calls

Barry's Diary: Sunday, March 20. 5:48 a.m.

The sun isn't up yet, but the sky is getting lighter. I haven't slept much. Every time I fall asleep, I hear that girl calling for Lucy. Is she the ghost who undid Lucy's leash? Did she take her away?

Lucy is snoring at the foot of my bed. She doesn't seem scared anymore. So I guess I shouldn't be worried.

Outside my window I can see the hill that leads up to the chapel. But I can't see the chapel. It's blocked by all the trees. A few minutes ago, a skunk came slowly down the path. It walked past our yard. Then it ran out of sight.

Lucy is awake now. She stretched and whined.
I wonder how she'll feel about going back into the
cemetery today.

How did Lucy disappear?

Was she hiding in a cave?

I think that Alma grabbed her,

And took her to her grave.

Barry yawned and got dressed. He walked quietly downstairs to the kitchen. Lucy followed him.

"I'm going out, girl," Barry said.

Lucy wagged her tail. She wanted to go, too. So Barry clipped on her leash and slipped out the door.

They walked into the cemetery like they did every day. Everything seemed still and quiet. Then Barry heard a dog bark. It sounded far away. Lucy heard it, too. She lifted her ears and howled.

Barry froze as he heard another sound. It was that girl's voice.

"Lucy!" she called. "Lucy, where are you?"

Lucy stopped walking and looked up at Barry. That other dog barked again. Then the girl called for Lucy. The other dog seemed to reply.

"Maybe there's another dog named Lucy," Barry said. He turned up the hill toward the chapel. The girl's voice was coming from there. *Just like last night.*

When they reached the top of the hill, Barry knelt next to Lucy. He grabbed her collar and held tight. He didn't want her to slip away again. Or to be let loose by an unseen ghost!

"Lucy!" came the sad cry.

The other dog barked.

"I hear you, Lucy," called the girl. "Where are you?"

The dog barked twice. It was on the other side of the cemetery.

Barry stroked Lucy's neck. "You're

being a good girl," he said. Lucy listened as the girl and the dog called back and forth.

The morning became brighter. The calling and the barking grew softer. Soon Barry couldn't hear them at all.

"Very strange," Barry said. He'd have to talk to Mitch and the other Zombie Hunters about this. Lucy started pulling. She led Barry to the graves behind the chapel.

When they reached Alma Simmons's grave, she stopped. She sniffed the ground and the gravestone. Then she whimpered a little and sniffed again.

Lucy sneezed. It was a powerful sneeze that made her head shake. She licked Barry's hand and started to walk away.

Barry put his hand on the gravestone. It was warmer than he'd expected. The sun wasn't fully up yet. The stone should be cold.

What's going on here? Barry thought.

Lucy tugged, so Barry followed. They

walked down the hill toward home. Lucy needed her breakfast.

It was only six thirty, so Barry would have to wait before calling Mitch. Maybe he could send him an instant message. But Mitch was probably still sleeping.

He went to the computer and checked his buddy list. Mitch wasn't online. Nor were any of the other Zombie Hunters. So Barry read about his favorite subject: ghosts. There were articles from around the world by people who had seen them over the years. Ghosts often lived in castles, inns, and old houses. Usually they did no harm.

After an hour, he called Mitch.

"Did I wake you up?" Barry asked.

"Yeah, but that's okay," Mitch said. "What's going on?"

"Just some weird stuff in the cemetery. Some ghost girl keeps crying for Lucy."

"She's crying for your dog?" Mitch

asked.

"I'm not sure," Barry said. "I think the ghost took Lucy away last night. But I also think there's another Lucy. Every time the ghost called her name, we could hear a dog barking from somewhere else."

"Did your Lucy come back last night?"

"Yeah. After a few minutes." Barry peeked into the hallway to check on her. She was curled up on her bed, fast asleep. "We went back out there this morning and heard the ghost. She kept calling and calling. But she stopped when it got light out."

Mitch didn't reply right away.

"Are you still there?" Barry asked.

"Yeah. I was just thinking. There's been some zombie activity in that cemetery this week."

"I didn't hear about that," Barry said.

"I just heard last night," Mitch said. "Maybe it's connected to this ghost and her dog."

"How?"

"I don't know," Mitch said. "I'll come by. We'll check it out."

"Should we call the others?" Barry asked.

"Let's have a look first. I'll be there in a few minutes."

"Okay," Barry said. "But this doesn't seem very scary. It's kind of weird to hear a ghost's voice, but she seems harmless."

"She might be," Mitch said, "but from what I've heard about these zombies, they might be *harmful*."

Chapter 3:
Evidence

Barry felt uneasy as they walked into Marshfield Grove. Mitch had told him more about the zombies. They'd been seen walking around the cemetery late at night a few times that week.

"Who saw them?" Barry asked.

"A couple of people," Mitch said. "Not many. They were down near the river." Mitch pointed up the hill. The river was on the other side.

"Zombies turn up at night," Mitch said. "Like most dead things. So mostly we see evidence. You don't usually see the zombies themselves."

"But somebody did see them?" Barry asked.

"Yeah."

Marshfield Grove had steeper hills than the other three cemeteries. The graves were the oldest in town, too. Many were from the 1700s. Only a few were from the past 100 years.

The boys reached a large granite gravestone. It was taller than they were. It was as big around as a refrigerator, and was topped with a tall cross. In stark letters was the name Byron Mumford. Below it were the years of his birth and death: 1821—1887.

"I used to play here," Barry said, nodding to the stone. "When I was little. I made believe this gravestone was part of a fort." He laughed. "Fort Mumford."

Mitch tapped on the stone. "It's sturdy."

"I've always loved this cemetery," Barry said. "Great place to hang out. So peaceful. I bring Lucy here every day."

Something farther down the hill caught Barry's eye. It was gray and brown and furry. "What's there?" he said, pointing.

"Looks like a dead animal," Mitch said.

Barry picked up a stick. They walked down the steep bank.

"Gross!" Barry said, poking at the pile of fur with the stick. There were the bodies of three squirrels, a rabbit, and a couple of chipmunks. None of them had heads. Thick, gooey blood clung to the fur near their necks.

"Who would take their heads?" Barry said. "Why would they leave the rest?"

Mitch shook his head. "Zombies eat brains," he said. "That's what I've always heard." He pointed toward the pile of bodies. "I'd say that's pretty good evidence of zombies right there."

Barry looked around. They were in the darkest area of the cemetery, far from any roads or houses. The river was below them. It wasn't very wide, but it was icy cold. It was running swiftly because so much snow had melted recently.

Mitch tapped Barry on the arm. "Zombies only come out at night, remember?"

They backed away from the pile and sat on a rock wall next to the Mumford gravestone.

"What should we do?" Barry asked.

"Well, we probably need more evidence," Mitch said. "We'll come back tonight with the others. I'll call Amy. You see if Jared and Stan are back yet. They went camping with Jared's dad."

"I'll call them," Barry said.

"Maybe we can take some photos of the zombies. Otherwise nobody will believe us. They'd think a bear dumped those bodies, or a trapper."

"And only took the heads?" Barry asked.

Mitch shrugged. "Like I said, we need solid evidence. A pile of little furry animals doesn't signal zombies. At least not to the police."

Barry shivered. "It does to me."

They stood up. A dog barked. It sounded close by, and it sounded scared.

"Where are you?" Barry said. "Here, boy."

The dog barked again. It seemed to be right on the hill, but Barry couldn't see it.

"Come on, boy," Barry called again.

The dog woofed. Then it howled.

"Where is it?" Mitch said. "It sounds like it's right there."

Barry walked down the slope again. He passed the dead animals. He could hear the dog whining, but there was no sign of it. Was it a ghost dog? Was it Alma's dog, the other Lucy?

"This is really strange," Mitch said. "I think the zombies have the dog."

"Right here?"

"Seems like it."

Barry thought about his dog. She'd been loose in this cemetery last night. He was so glad she was safe. The zombies could have grabbed her and eaten her brain. He'd be sure to keep her safe until this zombie scare was over.

But what about the dog they kept hearing? Was it in danger?

"We have to save that dog," Barry said.

"I know," Mitch said. "But how? We can't even see it."

"Tonight," Barry said. "If it's a ghost dog, maybe we'll be able to see it then."

Mitch nodded. "That may be our only chance. If the ghosts and the zombies operate at night, then that's what we need to do, too."

"It sounds dangerous, but we have to,"

Barry said.

"Yep," Mitch agreed. "Zombies start out by eating little brains, but then they move on to bigger ones. Your brain might be next!"

Barry's Diary: Sunday, March 20. 10:35 a.m.

So here's the plan. We'll hit the cemetery tonight after dark. If we can rescue that dog, we will. But we have to do more than that. I don't want those zombies killing little animals either. It's one thing if a bobcat or a coyote kills a rabbit or a squirrel. That's natural. Big, meat-eating animals have every right to eat. But not zombies. They're already dead! We have to stop them.

>Missing dog.
>
>Sad ghost.
>
>Have to help them
>
>Or I'll be toast.

I'll have to take Lucy for a long run this afternoon to tire her out. I don't want her going with us tonight. Too dangerous. I don't mind danger myself. But I can't take the risk of losing her.

Chapter 4:
Zombie Sighting

Lucy whined and stamped her feet as Barry headed for the door that evening.

"I won't be gone long, Lucy," Barry said. He patted her head.

"She wants you to take her," said his mom.

"I know," Barry said. "But Mitch's mother doesn't like having a dog in the house. Too much shedding. So Lucy has to stay home."

He felt bad for Lucy as he walked away from the house. When he looked back, she was staring out the window.

She knows where I'm going, Barry thought. *She always does.*

He walked up the dark street for about half a block. Then he heard Mitch's voice.

"Over here." Mitch and Amy were sitting on a low wall in front of a house.

"Do you guys have flashlights?" Barry asked.

"Yeah," said Amy.

"I hope you're wearing sneakers," Barry said. "We may have to run."

"Did you get ahold of Stan or Jared?" Mitch asked.

"Nope," Barry said. "I left messages."

They stood up and started walking toward the entrance of the cemetery.

"So, how do we rescue this dog?" asked Amy.

Barry shrugged. "I don't know yet. I was hoping we'd get an idea when we actually see it. So far we've only heard barking."

They didn't have to wait long. They could hear several dogs barking as they entered the cemetery. They also heard the lonely ghost's voice calling for her dog.

"Lucy!" came the eerie call. "Where are you, Lucy?"

Amy stopped walking. "Who was that?" she asked.

"Didn't Mitch tell you?" Barry said.

"Tell me what?" Amy said. "He told me we were trying to save a lost dog."

"We are," Barry said. "But we're trying to save it from some zombies."

Amy frowned. "I would like to have known that in advance."

"That isn't all," said Mitch. "That girl calling for Lucy is a ghost."

"We think it's a ghost," said Barry. "We haven't seen her."

The voice called again, and the dog answered with several loud barks.

"She sure sounds like a ghost," said

Amy. "She lost her dog?"

"We think the zombies snatched it," Barry said. "Otherwise the dog would come back to her. It sounds like it wants to. We think the zombies have it trapped."

Amy shook her head. "So all we have to do is wipe out the zombies and set the dog free?" she said. "I'm sure that will be easy." Amy rolled her eyes.

"We never said it would be easy," Mitch replied.

"Zombies kill people," Amy said. "They have super strength and they don't feel any pain."

"That's because they're dead," Barry said.

"Exactly." Amy let out a sigh. "They kill people and turn them into more zombies. Pretty soon there are more zombies than you can count."

"That's why we have to wipe them out," Mitch said. "Before they kill us. Or those dogs."

There were several dogs howling now. They could still hear the girl calling for Lucy. Every time the dog heard its name, it barked. And then the other dogs barked, too.

A tiny, high shriek came from down the hill. Barry turned his flashlight toward the sound. A huge man with sunken eyes was staring at them. In his fist was a gray squirrel, trying to get free.

"It's a zombie!" Mitch said.

"Drop that squirrel!" said Barry.

The zombie moaned. He lifted the squirrel to his mouth, then bit it. He shook his head as he chewed. When he pulled his hand away, the squirrel had no head.

"Gross!" said Barry.

Blood was dripping from the zombie's mouth.

"Go back where you came from!" shouted Amy.

The zombie started walking toward

them. He was slow and he wobbled from side to side as he moved.

"Let's get out of here!" said Mitch. They ran toward the chapel.

"That guy was ugly!" Amy said as they ran.

"And mean!" Mitch said. "He'd bite off our heads if he had the chance."

They reached the chapel and stopped. Each Zombie Hunter stopped to catch their breath.

"Stay close together," Barry whispered. "There could be more zombies anywhere."

They went to the back of the chapel and leaned against the wall. All was quiet back there. They kept their flashlights off while they rested. The night was very dark.

Barry took a deep breath and let it out. "She stopped."

"Who did?" asked Amy.

"The ghost. She's not calling for Lucy."

"Maybe we scared her," Mitch said.

Barry stared at the gravestone of Alma Simmons. A strange white light was beginning to form into a shape. It floated above the grave. Soon Barry could tell that it was a girl.

"I don't think we scared her at all," Barry said softly. He nudged Mitch's arm and pointed toward the grave. "She's right over there!"

Chapter 5:
Meet Alma

"**A**re you Alma?" Barry said, taking a few steps back from the grave. He'd seen ghosts before, but he'd never spoken to one who was close to his age.

"Yes, I am," the ghost said. "Do you have my Lucy?"

"No," Barry replied. "Is that her barking?"

"Yes." The ghost turned toward the sound. "Lucy!" she called. "Come back!"

"We think she's been taken," Barry said. "How long has she been missing?"

"I don't know," said Alma. "She's been with me for a long, long time. Recently she left my side." Alma's clothing, hair, and body were all white. Barry could see through her. She wasn't solid, but her shape was clear.

"What kind of dog is she?" Barry asked. "What color?"

"She's white," Alma said. "With a streak of gold."

"That sounds like my dog," Barry said. "Her name is Lucy, too. Did you see her last night?"

"Your dog came to me when I called for my Lucy," Alma said. "She is very sweet. But I want my dog back."

"We'll try to get her," Barry said. "But . . . she's a ghost dog, right?"

Alma stared at Barry. Then she turned away. The dogs were still barking on the other side of the cemetery. Alma looked that way.

"Lucy has been with me for many, many years," she said. "She's been my dog since I was six years old."

"We'll find her," Barry said. "We'll bring her back to you."

"Please do."

"I have one more question," Barry said. "Did you unhook my dog from her leash last night?"

Alma didn't answer. Instead, she began to fade. Soon they couldn't see her anymore. Barry waved Amy and Mitch closer.

"I don't think Alma knows that her dog is a ghost," Barry said. "So, maybe Alma doesn't realize that's she's dead, too."

"Most ghosts don't realize that," Mitch said. "They're kind of stuck in one place. They're searching for something."

"But Alma died a long time ago," Barry said. "I think she's been at peace since then. I never heard her until last night."

"At least she's had Lucy for company all these years," Amy said. "It must be awful to lose someone you've been so close to."

"We have to bring her dog back," Barry said. "She'll never be able to rest again unless we do."

"How do we do that?" asked Amy.

Barry shook his head. "I don't know yet. But we're smarter than those zombies. We'll figure out how to do this."

Barry led the way as they walked toward the sound of the dogs. He told Amy what he and Mitch had seen that afternoon.

"There were lots of dead animals," he said. "But when the squirrels and rabbits are gone, the zombies might start eating those dogs. We have to stop them soon."

"They'll try to kill us, too," Mitch said. "Stay close together and be ready to run."

Barry stepped carefully. He shined his light ahead. He tried to figure out how many dogs he could hear. There were at least four different barks. There had only been one before. Had the zombies trapped more dogs? Or were the new ones just barking because they heard the other one?

"Let's go down to the river," he whispered. "We'll work our way along the bank. Then we'll climb toward that Mumford gravestone."

"Is that where the dogs are?" Amy asked.

"We think so," Barry said. "We heard one this afternoon but we couldn't see it."

The bank of the river was muddy and overgrown with bushes. They had to move slowly. As they came around a big twist in the river, Barry heard a groan. He lifted his light and saw that he was face-to-face with a zombie. It was only ten feet away!

"Get back!" Barry yelled, taking several quick steps backward. The zombie stayed put, but it was staring at him. It had huge shoulders and several bloody spots on its head. Most of its teeth were missing.

"It's not alone," said Amy. She shined her light to the zombie's left, where a smaller one with only one eye was standing. It was holding a dead animal in its hand. The striped tail was long enough to reach the ground. The animal's head was broken open.

A third zombie was standing behind them. It was the one they'd seen earlier on the other side of the cemetery. Bloody drool was dripping from its mouth.

The zombies each took a step forward. They looked hungry and mean.

Barry gripped his flashlight tighter. He wished he had another weapon. He glanced back. Then to the side. He, Mitch, and Amy were trapped on a small bit of land. The river curved behind them, and around them on both sides.

The only way out was in front of them. Right where the zombies were standing!

Chapter 6:
A Trap

"**D**on't panic," Barry said. He grabbed Mitch's and Amy's arms. They took two steps back, up to the edge of the river.

The zombies stepped forward. One of them let out an awful groan.

Barry gripped his flashlight. He'd throw it if he had to. He took another step back. His foot landed in the water. It soaked right through his sneaker and made Barry shiver.

"We have nowhere to go," Amy said.

"Yes, we do," Mitch replied. He nodded

toward the river.

"We'd drown," said Amy.

"Just wait," Barry said. He shined the light into the front zombie's eyes. The zombie just stared at the beam. But it stopped walking.

"Lock your lights on the others!" Barry said.

The beams seemed to freeze the zombies, who just stared and groaned. They didn't even blink with the bright lights in their eyes. But they didn't move forward either.

"My feet are freezing!" Mitch said.

All three kids were standing in the river now. The water was only up to their ankles. But Barry knew that it dropped off steeply. If they took another step, they'd be up to their waists. That cold water would shock them quickly. They'd be in great danger of being swept away and drowning.

Barry turned his light slightly. The zombie followed the beam with its eyes.

"We can shift them," he whispered.

Mitch and Amy nodded. They changed the angle of their beams, too. The zombies moved a bit as they followed the light. They seemed confused.

There was very little room for the three Zombie Hunters to escape, but at least there was a bit more now. If they could distract the zombies, they might be able to slip past them and run.

Barry had an idea. "Lucy!" he called.

From very nearby, a dog barked. *I was right,* Barry thought. *That's Alma's dog.*

"Hi, Lucy!" Barry called again. "Good girl."

The ghost dog howled. Then several other dogs started barking, too. The zombies heard the barking. They turned and looked behind them.

"Run!" Barry yelled.

He, Mitch, and Amy scooted past the zombies. They climbed up the bank as fast as they could. The zombies tried to chase them, but they slipped in the mud.

"Faster!" Barry called. Branches scraped his forehead as he ran. Mitch tripped over a root and fell to his knees. Amy raced ahead as Barry grabbed Mitch's arm and helped him up. The zombies were almost on top of them.

They ran past the Mumford gravestone and many others, finally reaching a clear path. Barry had never run harder in his life. His breath was short and rapid.

"Keep going!" Barry yelled. "We'll rest at the chapel."

Soon they were way ahead of the zombies. *Maybe they won't even follow us,* Barry thought. But he kept running.

When they reached the chapel, Barry shined his light on Alma's grave. There was no sign of her. He felt the gravestone and it was cold. He let out his breath and started walking toward home.

Mitch and Amy fell in step with him. They all were puffing and sweating.

"Did you get hurt?" Barry asked Mitch.

"I just cut my hand," Mitch replied. "No big deal. You?"

Barry wiped his hand across his forehead. His fingers came away dotted with blood. "A few scrapes. How about you, Amy?"

"Just scared to death," she said. Then she smiled. "Almost to death. That was a little more dangerous than rescuing a lost dog. You left out a few details, Mitch."

"Sorry," Mitch said. "I didn't want to scare you off before we even started."

They reached the street and Barry stopped walking. "Did you see what that short zombie was holding?" he asked. "It was a dead raccoon. They're killing larger animals now. We have to stop them."

"We need more help," Mitch said. "There are three of them. Three of us."

"We'll make sure Jared and Stan come

with us tomorrow night," Barry said. "We have to get rid of those zombies by then. I don't want them killing dogs. Or cats. My neighbors' cats are out in that cemetery all the time!"

"So far they're just killing wild animals," Amy said. "That's terrible, but at least they haven't killed any pets. Not that we know of."

"But they've got those dogs trapped somehow," Barry said. "It's only a matter of time. We need to act fast. Tomorrow night is the deadline. Are you guys with me?"

"I am," said Mitch.

"Count me in," Amy said.

"They have to be stopped," Barry said. "It's scary and it's dangerous. But this is way too important not to take action."

Barry's Diary: Sunday, March 20. 9:51 p.m.

We barely escaped. We weren't smart. We walked right into their trap. We'll be much more careful tomorrow night.

There seems to be only three zombies. That's a good thing. But zombies kill people and turn them into zombies, too. So if we don't get rid of these three, there will be more. And I could be one of them! That's a scary thought. I don't want to kill anything, but maybe it's me or them. I don't want to spend the rest of my nights stumbling around in a cemetery. Biting the heads off squirrels. Or people!

If I was a zombie

I'd have a lot of worries.

Aren't there any zombies

Who only eat berries?

There are two things we must do. Get rid of the zombies. And get Alma's dog back for her so she can rest in peace.

Chapter 7:
Gathering Information

On Monday, all five Zombie Hunters got to school early. They met on the outdoor basketball court. Barry told Jared and Stan what had happened over the weekend.

"We need a plan," Barry said. "What do you know about zombies?"

"They'll infect anyone they bite," said Stan. "It could happen to any of us."

"We'll wear thick clothing," Barry said. "Put on a leather jacket if you have one."

"They're constantly hungry," Amy said.

"You saw what they did to that raccoon."

"They're killing raccoons now?" Stan asked. "That's bad. If they're killing bigger animals, it means they're getting hungrier."

"And more dangerous," said Amy.

Barry looked up at the basketball backboard. He was thinking hard. "That hunger could work in our favor," he said after a moment.

"How?" asked Mitch.

"I'm not sure," Barry said. "But it's worth remembering. Maybe we can take advantage of it."

Jared hadn't said much yet. Barry pointed to him. "Any ideas?" he asked.

"Are we going to try to kill these zombies?" Jared asked.

Barry raised both hands. "How else can we stop them?"

"Isn't there another way?" asked Amy.

"You mean besides killing them?" Mitch

asked. "Why is that a problem? They're already dead!"

"Not exactly," said Jared.

"Dead is dead," Mitch replied. "They're dead and they're killers. We have to wipe them out."

"I agree," said Barry. "They'll kill everything in that cemetery before too long. And then they'll start outside the cemetery. On people."

"You kill a zombie by bashing in its

brain," said Stan. "With a mallet or something."

Mitch sneered. "This isn't a video game," he said. "If we get violent with them, we're more likely to get hurt. Or killed. We have to outsmart them."

Barry pulled his notebook from his pocket. He always kept it there. He flipped through the pages until he found the next blank one.

"What is that?" Mitch asked.

"A diary." Barry blushed. "I mean a journal. I make notes in it about ghosts and stuff."

"A diary?" Mitch asked.

"A journal."

Mitch made his voice go high and squeaky. "Dear diary, last night I met this wonderful girl."

"Shut up."

"Her name was Alma," Mitch said. "She was dreamy!"

"Don't make fun of ghosts," Barry said.

"I'm making fun of you."

"Cut it out. This is serious business."
Barry began to write. "We need to get our
plan started."

Barry's Diary: Monday, March 21. 8:09 a.m.

Zombies:

- strong
- angry
- hungry
- stupid
- killers

How to stop them:

- bash their brains
- ?

"Any better ideas?" Barry asked.

"I read online that you can kill them by
making them eat salt," Jared said.

"Plain old salt?" Mitch asked.

"Yeah. A lot of it."

"Wait a minute," said Stan. "I read that salt makes them even stronger. Does that make sense?"

"I don't think it would make them stronger," Amy said. "Sugar might. But salt? It melts ice. It dries out your mouth if you eat a lot. It makes you thirsty. I don't know how it would kill a zombie. But most of what it does in your body is bad for you."

"We have a ton of salt in the garage," Barry said. "My dad throws it on the driveway when it's icy." He crossed out the question mark in his diary and wrote *feed them salt*.

"It might work," he said. "Any other ideas?"

They talked about other things they'd read or heard about zombies. How they couldn't run fast, but they could grab you quickly. That they smelled like rotten meat. They made inhuman noises. You could sometimes get away from one by bonking it on the nose.

Barry wrote everything down in his diary. "Good start," he said. "We'll meet at eight tonight at the entrance to Marshfield Grove. Bring flashlights and something to protect yourself with. I'll work out a plan."

Barry looked at his notes. They weren't much help yet. He still had no idea how to stop the zombies.

But he had to make it happen tonight.

Chapter 8:
Salt in the Wound

Barry's Diary: Monday, March 21. 4:42 p.m.

They've had their chance. That's how I see it. The zombies already lived once. Now they're taking away other lives. That's not fair.

I have a plan. I'll bring Lucy out to the cemetery after I set up some things. But I'll leave her home tonight.

Lucy is a nut.

She barks and howls and whines.

I wonder how she'd help to fight

The zombies in the pines.

"I'll be back for you soon," Barry said to Lucy. He found his old red wagon in the garage. He loaded it with three big bags of rock salt and headed for the cemetery.

The salt was heavy. It was hard to pull the wagon up the hill. But he needed to do it. What he was about to do would be much worse.

The afternoon was cloudy. It would be a dark night. Barry gulped. His task would be hard. At least he'd have the other Zombie Hunters to help.

When he reached the Mumford grave, he tore open a bag of salt. Then he looked around. He didn't have to look far.

Several dead animals were on the hill in the woods. Barry put on a pair of leather gloves. That might keep his hands clean. But the smell was awful. He wished he had a mask.

He picked up a couple of squirrels and a rabbit. They'd all been chewed. Parts of their heads were missing. He walked back to the wagon.

This is disgusting, Barry thought. But he had to do this. He spread apart the pieces of the rabbit's head. Then he poured salt into the opening. He pressed it shut. He did the same thing to the squirrels, stuffing them with all the salt they could hold. He still had two bags left.

Barry gagged. The smell was so bad that he thought he might throw up. But he kept working.

Soon he had ten small animals piled in the wagon. They all were loaded with salt. He wheeled the wagon to the side of the Mumford gravestone.

I need a few more, he thought. The animals that were still scattered about this area had been chewed too well. Their heads were gone. He'd have to look farther.

The side of the hill was steep. Barry made his way down carefully. He had to use his hands to grab branches and rocks so he wouldn't fall. But he could see a pile of dead chipmunks.

When he reached the pile, he noticed a pit in the side of the hill. The hole was about six feet across and ten feet deep. It was covered with thick branches, but he could see down into it. It seemed empty.

Two of the dead chipmunks had not been eaten at all. Barry carried them back to the wagon. He stuffed their mouths full of salt. Then he walked home. He couldn't wait to shower. His gloves were coated with blood and slime.

That's the grossest thing I've ever done, he thought. Worse than when he'd puked down the front of his shirt on a roller coaster. Worse than the time he'd taken a bite of an apple and bit a worm in half.

I hope it will be worth it, he thought. *If it gets rid of those zombies, it will be.*

But would the zombies eat the animals from the wagon? They'd already eaten parts of them. And they'd thrown away the rest. Maybe if they get hungry enough. Or if we can trick them somehow.

After a long, hot shower, Barry took Lucy back to the cemetery. They walked up toward the chapel. Lucy seemed very excited. It was after six thirty. Much later than their usual walk.

"What do you smell?" Barry asked.

Lucy pulled harder on the leash.

"Do you smell those stupid zombies?" Barry asked. "After tonight they'll be gone."

At least I hope so, he thought.

Lucy stopped to sniff a gravestone. Barry kept walking. He tugged on the leash. "Let's go, girl," he said. "I'm getting hungry. I haven't had dinner yet."

When he looked back, Lucy's leash was dragging on the ground. She was gone!

"Lucy!" he yelled. He didn't see her. Thoughts of zombies and ghosts came to his mind. "Lucy!" he called even louder.

This is crazy, Barry thought. He looked around in fear. *Where could she have gone?*

Barry ran the rest of the way up the hill until he reached the chapel. "Lucy!" he yelled. "Come here, girl!"

There was no sign of her. He couldn't hear her tags. She was gone.

Barry felt helpless. Had the zombies snatched her? But he would have seen them. Did Alma take her again? That was probably it.

Barry went straight to Alma's grave. It was quiet there. "Alma?" Barry said. "Do you have my dog?"

There was no response. Barry looked around. "Lucy?" he said. "Come here, please."

But she didn't come running this time. Barry called her name again. Then he ran down the hill toward home. He needed help. He had to get ahold of Mitch.

He had to get Lucy back before the zombies ate her.

Chapter 9:
A Plea for Help

The sun had gone down by the time Barry and Mitch reached the chapel. It was seven thirty. The dogs had already started barking. Alma would start calling soon.

Barry walked in a wide circle, calling Lucy's name. Mitch was carrying a baseball bat in case a zombie attacked him. He went down the other side of the hill and called for Lucy, too.

Barry wasn't sure where Lucy was. He thought she must be trapped with the other dogs somewhere near the Mumford gravestone. Maybe in that pit. But he kept looking over by the chapel. He didn't want to go back where the zombies were until all of the Zombie Hunters arrived.

After twenty minutes, Mitch came back.

"No sign of her?" Barry asked.

Mitch shook his head. "No," he said. "But don't worry. We'll find her."

"I'm not leaving this graveyard until we do," Barry said.

"Me either," Mitch said. "But I need to go meet the others by the entrance. Do you want to stay here?"

"Yeah. I'll see you in a few minutes."

Barry stood still. He could hear the other dogs barking. It didn't sound as if Lucy was with them. But maybe she was. When the others got here, they would go back to the Mumford area to check.

With Mitch gone, Barry sat on the chapel steps and took out his notebook.

Barry's Diary: Monday, March 21. About 7:50 p.m.

> The zombies stole my dog.
> We're planning an attack.
> There will be no funny poems
> Until Lucy has come back.

Barry walked around the chapel again. As he turned the corner, he stopped in his tracks. Alma was floating right in front of him. She was glowing softly.

"You've lost your dog, too?" she asked.

"Yes," Barry said. "I thought maybe you had her again."

"Now both Lucys are missing."

"Can you help me find them?"

Alma looked down. "I've never gone away from this spot," she said sadly. She waved her arm around the little graveyard behind the chapel. "Not in many, many years."

"Do you think you can try?" Barry asked.

"We'll be with you. Me and my friends. We think the dogs are trapped on the other side of the cemetery."

Alma turned her head to look down the hill. Then she pointed to her grave. "This is my resting place," she said. "Right here. My place of peace."

"I know," Barry said. "It's a very nice spot. Quiet and shaded. But I need your help."

Barry gulped. How could he ask Alma to leave her grave? She'd been there for more than 150 years. But they might never get their dogs back unless she helped. She was the one who knew the spirit world. She might cross into the world of the undead and overcome those zombies.

"I'll stay by your side if you come with us," Barry said.

"Please try without me," Alma said. "I'll be right here."

Alma slowly faded from sight. Barry sat

down again. He put his head in his hands and waited for Mitch and the others. He thought about his dog.

Lucy had been a tiny puppy when they first took her home. So cute, with big paws and sweet, trusting eyes. For seven years now, she'd been by his side. She slept in his room every night. They took walks in this graveyard twice a day. Lucy loved him. And he loved her. He wiped a tear from his eye.

Barry sat there for ten minutes. Then he heard a sound.

It was a groan. An awful, moaning groan. The kind of sound only a zombie could make.

And it was coming from the other side of the chapel.

Chapter 10:
The Guard

Barry stood and stared at the corner of the chapel, waiting for the zombie to appear. But all was quiet again.

"Mitch?" Barry said. "Was that you?"

There was no reply.

Barry's stomach rumbled. He hadn't eaten any dinner.

"Mitch?" he said again. "Amy?"

He was alone. At least, he was the only living person around. He bent down and picked up a rock the size of a baseball.

"Alma," he said softly, "are you here?"

Suddenly a zombie stepped around the corner. It was the one with huge shoulders and very few teeth. It stopped when it saw Barry and moaned.

"Where's my dog?" Barry said.

The zombie swung an arm to punch Barry and took a step forward. Barry stepped back. The zombie was several feet away. Barry could easily run away if he had to.

"I said, where's my dog?" Barry asked again. He lifted the rock, ready to throw.

The zombie stayed still, glaring at Barry. He was wearing an old gray shirt, stained with blood and dirt and yellow goo. His hair was greasy and lay flat on his head.

Barry took a small step forward, hoping the zombie would be scared. But the zombie didn't move. So Barry stepped back again.

A strong, slimy hand grabbed Barry's arm. When he turned, Barry saw that he was in the grip of the shorter zombie. The zombie's breath was foul and his one eye looked blank. But he squeezed hard and Barry was stuck.

"Let go!" Barry yelled. He saw the other zombie coming toward him. With his free arm Barry lifted the rock and swung it at the shorter zombie's face. He felt a squish as the rock hit the zombie's nose. The zombie groaned. He let go of Barry's arm. Barry twisted loose and stumbled away, falling on Alma's grave.

The two zombies bumped into each other. Barry had just enough time to crawl to his feet and escape. The zombies ran after him, but they were much slower.

Barry wasn't sure where to run. But then he remembered that Mitch and the others would be heading for the chapel. He had to warn them. So he ran toward the entrance of the cemetery.

He could see them coming up the path.

"Over here!" he shouted. "Hurry!"

Mitch, Amy, and Stan ran over.

"Where's Jared?" Barry asked.

"His parents wouldn't let him out," Stan said. "What's going on? You look frantic."

"One of the zombies grabbed me," Barry said. "They were up by the chapel."

"All three of them?" Mitch asked.

"I only saw two," Barry said. "But if we move quickly, we can get to those dogs before they do. Even if the other one is still there. With four of us, we should be able to outwit it."

They ran toward the other side of the graveyard. They could hear the dogs barking. Barry strained to hear Lucy. But he wasn't sure if he did. There were too many barks at once.

"Spread out a bit," Barry said as they slowed down. "Not too much. If one of us gets caught, the others can rescue him."

"Or her!" said Amy.

"You know what I mean," Barry said. "Keep your flashlights on so we know where everybody is."

They walked to the Mumford grave. Barry shined his light around. The wagon was still there. None of the dead animals had been taken from it.

There was no sign of the third zombie.

Barry pointed to the slope. "The dogs are over there," he said. He could hear them whining and howling.

"Lucy?" Barry called. "Are you there?"

One dog answered. It sounded like Alma's dog. Barry let out his breath. Where was his Lucy?

The rest of the dogs started barking, too.

"There's a big hole in the woods," Barry said. "It's covered up with branches. It was empty earlier today, but I think the dogs are there."

"Then where were they during the day?" Stan asked.

"These are ghost dogs, remember?" Barry said. "Except for my Lucy."

She'd better not be a ghost dog, he thought. His eyes began to sting with tears. He sniffed and made a fist. "Let's look," he said. He led the way down the slope.

As they got closer, Barry was sure that he'd found the right place. The dogs were yelping and howling.

Barry shined his light on the branches that covered the pit. The barking grew louder.

"We found them!" Mitch said.

Barry handed Amy his flashlight. He bent to grab one of the branches. "Get that end," he said to Stan.

They picked up the branch and set it aside. Then they pulled away some other brush.

"Are you in there, Lucy?" Barry asked.

Several dogs barked, but none of them sounded like his Lucy.

As Barry reached for another branch, a hand reached from behind and gripped his arm.

"He's got me!" Barry yelled. He pulled back but the zombie held tight.

The zombie began to back up into the woods, dragging Barry by the arm.

"Hit him!" Barry said. "Make him let me go!"

Stan shoved one of the branches at the zombie. Mitch whacked him in the shoulder with his baseball bat. Amy picked up a handful of stones and threw them.

Barry pulled hard and yanked his arm free. As he turned to run, he saw the other two zombies coming close.

"That way!" Barry yelled, pointing up the far side of the slope and running. Stan, Mitch, and Amy ran, too. The dogs barked louder. The zombies groaned and spit.

I guess they left one zombie there to guard the dogs, Barry thought. His plan had almost worked. But the zombies were a little smarter than he'd thought.

"What now?" Mitch asked as they reached a safe spot.

Barry shook his head. "We're not giving up," he said. "Those dogs have to be set free. And we have to find my dog, too. I won't sleep until I get her back. I'll stay in this cemetery all night if I have to."

Mitch nodded. "You might have to," he said. "I won't strand you."

Barry looked at Amy and Stan. "How about you guys?" he asked.

Stan looked at his watch. "I've got another half hour," he said.

Amy shrugged. "Me too," she said. "It's a school night. Sorry."

Barry took a deep breath and let it out. "Let me think," he said.

He hoped time wasn't running out for Lucy.

Chapter 11:
Now What?

Barry's Diary: Monday, March 21. 8:52 p.m.

The zombies have the pit surrounded. They know we want to free those dogs. Stan and Amy have to leave soon. It will be up to me and Mitch. I'm supposed to be in by 10, but I won't go home without Lucy.

I don't know where she could be. I didn't hear her in the pit. I'd know her bark anywhere. Could the zombies have eaten her? That would be the worst thing that's ever happened to me.

So what do we do now? We have to get those zombies away from the dogs. And we have to keep searching for Lucy.

B arry was getting very hungry. "Do you guys have anything to eat?"

"Sure," Mitch said with a laugh. "I've got a picnic basket right here. What do you want? A turkey sandwich? Some chicken?"

"Very funny," Barry said. "I didn't have dinner. I was hoping somebody had a candy bar in their pocket or something."

"Nope," said Stan.

"Sorry," said Amy.

"Do you like raw chipmunk brains?" Mitch asked.

Barry scowled. "That's not funny," he said. "Don't be a jerk."

"Sorry, man," Mitch said. "I was just trying to lighten things up. This isn't easy."

Barry let out his breath and stared at the ground.

"We'll find her," Mitch said. But he didn't sound very hopeful.

Stan and Amy left a few minutes later.

They promised to come back right after school tomorrow.

"My parents would ground me if I stayed out too late," Amy said.

"Me too," said Stan.

Barry rubbed his hands together and pulled up his sweatshirt hood. The night wasn't too cold, but they'd been sitting still for a while.

Mitch and Barry walked toward the Mumford grave. They knew that they couldn't get close. They just wanted to see if the zombies were still there.

They were.

"Now what?" Mitch asked. "With only two of us, we'd be in real danger if we went down there."

"I know," Barry said. "But Lucy's the one in danger now. And the rest of those dogs."

"We need a good plan," Mitch said.

"I'm thinking." Barry looked back

toward the chapel. "We need help from Alma."

"What can she do?" Mitch asked. "She's a ghost."

"Exactly," Barry said. "She knows the world of the dead."

"Does she? You said she's never left that graveyard. It's just been her and her dog all these years."

"Right," Barry said. "But she's been dead."

"At peace."

The dogs started howling even louder than before. They sounded scared and frantic.

From the other side of the cemetery, another dog barked, too.

"That sounded like my Lucy!" Barry said.

The bark had come from the area near the chapel. Barry started running toward it.

"Lucy?" he called.

They reached the chapel and shined their lights around. There was no sign of any living creature. And the dog had stopped barking.

"Are you sure that was her?" Mitch asked.

"I think so," Barry said. "I only heard one bark. But it sounded like her."

"Lots of dogs sound alike," Mitch said.

Barry shined his light at Alma's grave. "I know," he said. "But I know my dog better than anything."

Mitch put his hand on Barry's shoulder. "There are lots of dogs in the neighborhood," he said softly. "And they all bark."

Barry pulled his shoulder away. "It was her."

"I hope so," Mitch said. "Call her again."

"Lucy!"

There was no reply.

"Alma?" Barry said this time. "Are you

here?"

Alma didn't reply either.

"Maybe we have to solve this on our own," Barry said. "Where's your baseball bat?"

Mitch sighed. "I don't know. I must have left it back by the pit. I didn't have much time to think when those zombies attacked us."

"We need more weapons."

"I know," Mitch said. "And I should check in at home. I'll sneak back out as soon as I can. Meet me right here."

"Okay," Barry said. His parents would be wondering where he was by now anyway. "I'll sneak out, too. And when I come back, I'm not leaving until this is over. We'll either finish off the zombies or they'll finish me."

Chapter 12:
Sneaking Out

Barry walked quietly through his backyard. His parents had been out at a meeting when he left the house earlier. They were back now. Barry could see the car in the driveway. There were several lights on downstairs.

Barry had done this before. He jumped up and grabbed a branch of a maple tree in the yard. Then he pulled himself up. He climbed until he could reach the roof over the side porch. Then he eased himself onto the roof.

He felt nervous but excited. He didn't want his parents to hear him.

His bedroom window was just a few feet away. Very slowly, Barry pushed the window up. Then he climbed through and onto his bed.

The hallway was dark. Barry tiptoed across to the bathroom. He hoped his parents hadn't been home for very long.

He turned on the shower and waited a few minutes. Then he opened the door and called down the stairs. "Hi, Mom! Hi, Dad!"

"Hi, Barry," his dad said. "We wondered where you were."

"I didn't hear you come in," Barry said. "When did you get here?"

"About fifteen minutes ago," his mom said.

"I had the shower running," Barry said. He was careful not to tell an actual lie. "I'm pretty tired now."

"Well, sleep tight," his dad called.

"I will."

Barry waited in his room for a while. He heard his parents come up the stairs and go to their bedroom.

He took out his diary.

Barry's Diary: Monday, March 21. 10:17 p.m.

I'm sure I heard Lucy before. She wasn't with the zombies. But where is she? She's lost or stuck. Maybe someone else has her trapped. Someone like Alma.

But maybe Mitch was right. Maybe that wasn't Lucy that I heard. She didn't respond when I called. Maybe she is in that pit. Maybe she's a ghost dog now.

No matter what I have to do tonight, I'm going to get in that pit. I'm going to release those dogs. And if Lucy isn't there, I'll keep looking until I find her.

Barry walked to his doorway and listened. His parents were quiet. He'd wait a little longer. Then he'd go back to

86

the cemetery.

He wanted to eat. But he also wanted his parents to think he was sleeping. *I'll eat later,* he thought. *Can't risk making any noise now.*

Barry took off his sweatshirt and put on a sweater. Then he put the sweatshirt on over it. He found a hammer in his closet and put it in the sweatshirt's big front pocket.

A few minutes later, he was back on the roof. He stepped very quietly. Then he reached for the branch, swung down, and dropped to the ground.

Outside the garage, he found a shovel. *This might come in handy,* he thought. The shovel was heavy and had a sharp metal blade. He didn't like the idea of hitting anything with it. Not even a zombie. But he needed protection. The shovel and the hammer might be enough.

Barry walked through the yard and into

the cemetery. He'd wait for Mitch near the chapel. And he'd try to talk to Alma first.

The sky had cleared by the time Barry reached the chapel. The moon was out. It was just a sliver, but it cast some light.

"Alma?" Barry said as he stood in front of her grave. "I know where your dog is."

There was no reply.

"Do you know where mine is?" Barry asked.

There was still no answer. But Barry thought he saw a flicker of light near the gravestone.

"Are you there?" he asked.

Slowly, Alma began to form. She floated above the grave. "Where is my Lucy?" she finally asked. She looked like a mist tonight. Very hard to see.

Barry pointed toward the river. "Down there," he said. "The zombies have her trapped. There are several dogs there."

Alma turned that way. "I want my Lucy

back," she said.

"And I want my Lucy, too," Barry said. "I think I heard her up here before. Was I wrong?"

"I don't know what you heard," Alma said.

"You don't have her with you?"

Alma grew brighter. She looked angry. But she didn't respond.

Barry stepped toward her. "Do you

know where my Lucy is?"

In a flash, Alma was gone.

"Oh, come on!" Barry said. "I need your help, Alma."

Barry drove the shovel into the ground next to Alma's grave. "Thanks for nothing," he said.

Barry folded his arms and stared at the gravestone. "I'm risking my life to save your dog, Alma," he said. "The least you could do is help me find mine."

Chapter 13:
Playing Chase

B arry was very upset when Mitch finally showed up.

"It's after eleven," Barry said. "What took you so long?"

Mitch was carrying a long metal rake. "My father was still up. He was watching a basketball game on TV. I couldn't sneak out until he went to bed."

"You need a better escape route," Barry said.

"Well, I'm here now," Mitch said. "I'm sure those zombies are still there. We've got all night."

Barry took the hammer out of his sweatshirt as he started to walk. "I don't want to take all night. I'm ready to end this now."

They walked silently for a few minutes. A breeze came up.

"Did you hear Lucy again?" Mitch asked.

Barry shook his head. "I think Alma has her. I don't know how that could be. She's a ghost! How can she trap a live dog?"

"Ghosts can do lots of things," Mitch said. "Things we can't even imagine."

"I asked her about it, but she vanished."

"Alma?" Mitch asked. "Was she here now?"

"Yeah. While I was waiting for you," Barry said. "I told her we needed her help. And I asked her where Lucy is. But she didn't help at all."

"I guess Alma is scared."

"So are we!" Barry shut off his flashlight. The moon gave enough light to see. He didn't want the zombies to have any idea they were coming.

"Quiet now," Barry said. "Let's sneak up on them."

They took a few slow steps.

"Wait," Barry said. "I forgot the shovel."

Mitch had the rake and Barry had his hammer.

"The baseball bat is still by the pit," Mitch said.

"Okay. I'll try to get that." Barry's stomach rumbled loudly.

"I thought you said to be quiet," Mitch whispered. He laughed.

"Can't help that," Barry said. "Forget it. Let's just hurry. All this running and walking is making it worse. I get hungrier every minute."

They reached the Mumford gravestone and knelt behind it. The zombies were down the hill near the pit. The dogs were barking, but not very much.

Barry looked at the wagon full of dead animals. It hadn't been touched.

"Those sure stink," Mitch said.

Barry started to push the wagon out to the front of the gravestone. "Maybe if they see it, they'll eat," he whispered. "If we're lucky, all that salt will ruin their brains."

The wagon's wheels squeaked. Barry stopped pushing. He heard the zombies groaning. They were coming toward him.

"Back up," Barry said. He and Mitch moved about twenty feet away. Barry held his hammer tight.

One of the zombies bent over the wagon and sniffed. Then he looked directly at Barry and Mitch. The dogs started howling. Then the zombie charged.

Barry turned and ran up the hill. He could see all three zombies chasing, but they were slow.

"I have an idea," Barry said to Mitch. "Keep running, but not very fast."

"Why not?"

"Because we want them to chase us," Barry said. "When we run too fast, they stop. Let's let them chase. Tire them out. Try to make them hungry."

"They're always hungry!"

"I mean hungrier," Barry said. "Like me. I'm so hungry I'm even thinking about eating those rotten animals."

"I get it," Mitch said. He fell to the ground on purpose. "Oh no!" he shouted. "They'll catch me."

Mitch waited for the zombies to get close, then he got up and ran. Barry was running toward him.

Barry ran close to the zombies. They turned and went after him. Each time they got close, Barry would speed up. Mitch did the same thing. Soon they'd led the zombies all the way to the other side of the cemetery.

Barry could hear the zombies moaning and puffing. They kept chasing. He and Mitch kept darting away.

Barry ran fast as they reached the hill near the chapel. When he reached the top, he looked down.

A rabbit ran out of the brush. One of the zombies reached for it, but it got away.

Barry could tell that the zombies were angry. They stared at the spot where the rabbit had been. Then they turned and headed back toward the river.

"I think it worked," Barry said.

"What do you mean?" Mitch asked. "They're still walking. We didn't finish them off."

"We made them hungrier," Barry said. "They couldn't catch that rabbit. I think they're heading back for an easier meal."

"From the wagon?" Mitch asked.

"Let's hope so. They have to eat a lot of salt somehow."

Mitch laughed. "We could invite them over for a picnic."

"Right," Barry said with a smile. "Or we could get some take-out food."

But then Barry got serious. "The wagon trick has to work," he said. "I don't know any other way."

It's our best shot, Barry thought. *If that salt doesn't kill them, we may be out of options.*

Chapter 14:
Smart Thinking

Barry's Diary: Monday, March 21. Almost midnight.

We can see the zombies. They are eating the animals from the wagon! They must be very hungry, because they are eating the whole bodies—not just the heads. There's a ton of salt in them.

Barry sat next to a gravestone and watched. Soon the zombies stumbled around, then sat. And then they were on their backs, rolling from side to side.

"It's working!" Barry said. "The salt is getting to them already."

"I hope so," Mitch replied. "Maybe they're just tired."

The zombies stayed still. They didn't move even when the dogs started barking again.

"What do you think?" Barry said.

"I don't know," Mitch said. "It takes a lot to stop a zombie. But that salt seems to have done something to them."

"Now we have to free those dogs," Barry said. "But how do you get a ghost dog out of a pit?"

"Maybe we have to go down there."

"Into the pit?" Barry asked.

"Yeah." Mitch rubbed his chin. He was thinking hard. "Can we build some sort of platform? So the dogs can climb up and out?"

"Maybe." Barry thought about what they could use. They had a rake, a baseball bat, and a hammer. Plus all those branches and the wagon.

"We'll do the best we can," he said.

Slowly they walked toward the Mumford grave. The zombies weren't moving. Barry put a finger to his lips, telling Mitch to stay quiet. He picked up the two extra bags of salt and put them in the wagon.

The wagon still smelled awful. There was slime and blood everywhere. Barry didn't want to touch the handle, but there was no other way.

He pulled the wagon down the hill toward the pit. As he and Mitch got closer, the dogs barked louder.

"We're here, puppies," Barry whispered. "We're going to set you free."

They found the baseball bat and pushed away the branches. Barry shined his light into the hole. He could see four dogs. They were misty and he could see through them.

"They're all ghosts," he said. "Just like we thought."

A dog that looked a lot like Lucy was

howling the loudest. "That must be Alma's dog," Barry said. He thought about his own Lucy. He'd find her next.

The boys carefully put the branches into the hole, leaning them against the sides. Then they eased their way into the hole, bringing their tools and the wagon.

The dogs backed into a corner. They were afraid.

"Don't worry," Mitch said. "We're here to save you. We'll get you out."

It took a long time, but the boys propped up the branches and made a small platform. They set the wagon below it. It would be hard, but the dogs could climb into the wagon, then onto the platform. If they jumped from there, they could reach the top of the pit.

"Go ahead, Lucy," Barry said. "That's your way back to Alma."

The ghost dogs stared at the platform for several minutes. They sniffed the wagon.

Lucy wagged her tail. Then she stepped into the wagon and jumped onto the platform. She looked back. Another dog stepped up to the wagon.

Lucy dug her paws into the dirt. It took a great effort, but she climbed out of the hole. Barry could see her peeking over the edge. The second dog climbed out, too. Then the third.

The last dog stayed in the corner.

"I wish we could just carry him out with us," Barry said. "But you can't pick up a ghost."

The dog was small. It had a thick, furry coat and big ears.

"Come on, boy," Mitch said. "You can do it."

The dog walked to the wagon and stepped in. It looked up at the platform and whined.

"Maybe if we lifted the wagon," Barry said. "We can't lift the dog, but we can lift the wagon."

It worked. They put the wagon on the platform. But the dog would not go farther. The distance to the top of the hole was too high.

"That platform won't hold us," Mitch said. "How do we get him up higher?"

Barry picked up the rake. "We can boost it with this and the bat."

"We might tip it over," Mitch said.

"We have no choice."

Mitch stepped under the platform. He placed the bottom of the rake between the wagon's front wheels. Barry did the same with the baseball bat, placing it near the back. Very carefully, they pushed straight up. The wagon lifted like an elevator. And the dog jumped to freedom!

"We did it!" Barry said. He dropped the bat.

"Yes!" Mitch said. "That was great. Hard work and smart thinking."

Barry laughed. "Are we smart enough to get out?"

"No problem," Mitch said. "We aren't dogs. We can climb up the branches."

Barry shined his light around the hole. The dirt smelled good. He was tired and hungry, but he knew it wouldn't be hard to get out. Maybe this was almost over.

"Let's rest," Barry said. He turned over the wagon and sat between the wheels. He was covered with dirt and blood. He still needed to find his dog. But he felt very good about what they'd done so far.

"Ready?" Mitch asked.

Barry stood up. "Sure. We still have work to do."

"We'll find your Lucy," Mitch said. "I promise."

"We need to climb one at a time," Barry said. "I'll go first."

He grabbed two of the branches that they'd used for the platform. He leaned them against the wall. They were sturdy.

Barry checked his sweatshirt pocket. His flashlight was still there. "We'll come back for the tools another time," he said. Then he started to climb.

He dug his feet into the dirt and pulled hard with his arms. It took longer than he expected, but soon he could see out of the top. He grabbed a small tree trunk and started to pull himself up.

And then he heard a terrible moan.

The zombies were back! The salt hadn't finished them off. They were standing a few feet from the pit. Waiting for him!

One zombie reached for Barry. Barry hurried back down the branches.

"What's going on?" Mitch said.

"Big problem," Barry said. "We've got visitors. And they still look really hungry!"

Chapter 15:
The Pit

The boys sat in the dark for several minutes. They could hear the zombies walking around near the top of the pit.

"I guess they can't get down here," Barry said. "They're too clumsy."

"Right," Mitch said. "But we can't get out. They'd grab us for sure."

Barry pointed his light at the top of the hole. The zombie with one eye peeked over the edge. He was drooling a huge amount. It dripped into the pit.

"Smells like ocean water," Mitch said. "Very salty."

"That's good," Barry said. He could see the white liquid dripping out of the zombie's nose, too. "The salt is working. It just takes time."

He hoped he was right. The zombies had eaten a lot of salt. It was oozing out of them now. But they were still awake. They still looked hungry. Maybe the salt wouldn't stop them after all.

"It may be working a little," Mitch said. "But they still could kill us. What are we going to do?"

All three zombies were looking into the pit now. Barry could see the ooze.

"They're wondering where the dogs went," Mitch said. "They'll blame us."

"Too bad for them," Barry said. He shook a fist at the zombies. "We're not through with you!" he yelled. "We set the dogs free. And we'll finish you off next."

The one-eyed zombie groaned.

"What if they do come down here?" Mitch asked.

Barry picked up the baseball bat. "We'll fight them off."

Mitch grabbed the rake.

The zombies were walking in circles around the pit now. They kept their eyes on the boys. Several times Barry had to wipe salty drool from his face.

"Careful you don't get any of that in your mouth," Mitch said. "You can get infected from that just like a bite."

"I know. But that slime is everywhere."

"What should we do?" Mitch asked.

"Take our time," Barry said. "This won't be easy. But let's just wait. I hope that salt will keep weakening them."

"Do you think they ate enough to kill their brains?" Mitch asked.

Barry shrugged. "I stuffed ten pounds of salt into those animals," he said. "The zombies ate them all. That's more than three pounds of salt each."

Mitch nodded. "That's a lot."

"It's probably more salt than a thousand bags of potato chips," Barry said. "Think about that."

They heard a crash as the one-eyed zombie fell. He hung over the edge of the pit, halfway in and halfway out. His head and chest were hanging into the pit. He was trying to push back out, but seemed too weak.

Mitch and Barry backed against the wall of the pit. Barry gripped the baseball bat tight.

The zombie slipped a little farther into the pit. A huge wad of white gunk dripped out of his mouth.

The zombie groaned loudly. Then he fell face-first to the bottom of the pit.

He landed with a thud and rolled over. He didn't move or make any sound. The salty liquid oozed from his mouth, his nose, his ears, and even his eyes.

"I think he's dead," Mitch whispered. "Again."

Barry reached out with the baseball bat and pushed the zombie's shoulder. There was no response. The zombie just lay still with his mouth open.

Barry looked at Mitch. He shrugged. Then he grinned.

"One down?" Mitch said.

"Looks like it," Barry said.

He could hear the other two zombies as they circled the pit. They didn't seem to be slowing down. They groaned and moaned as they walked.

"Maybe this one ate most of the salt," Mitch said, pointing to the dead zombie with his rake.

"I don't think so," Barry said. "He's the smallest. So maybe it killed him faster."

Mitch looked up toward the top of the

pit. "I hope so," he said.

"Those others are oozing salt, too," Barry said. "It's just a matter of time."

They waited for about twenty minutes. Things were quiet now. They hadn't heard the other two zombies for several minutes.

Barry kept looking at the one-eyed zombie, who was lying on the floor of the pit. He hadn't moved at all. But what about the other two? Were they just waiting up there? The boys would have to leave the hole sometime. And it would be easy for the zombies to kill them as they climbed out.

Unless the zombies were already dead.

Dead again, Barry thought. *Let's hope so.*

Chapter 16:
Save Yourself!

Barry climbed very slowly to the top of the hole. He tried not to make any sound. He peeked over the edge. He didn't see any zombies.

"Are you okay?" Mitch said from below.

"It looks clear," Barry said. He climbed out. "Get up here."

Mitch was out in a few seconds. "What about the tools?" he said.

"Maybe we won't need them," Barry said. "If we're lucky, those zombies are lying somewhere near here—dead."

"Should we look for them?" Mitch asked.

"I suppose," Barry said. "Just to be sure."

Barry took his flashlight from his pocket and shined it around. The ground was covered in salty gunk. Still no zombies.

"This isn't good," Barry said. "If they were finished, we'd see them lying here."

"Do you think they walked away?" Mitch said.

Barry nodded. He shined the light in a wider circle. He didn't see them. He gulped. They were still in a lot of danger. The zombies could be anywhere. Behind any tree.

"Stick close together," Barry said. "Or should we spread out?"

The night was very dark. The hill they were on was steep. There were thick trees and bushes—lots of places for a zombie to hide.

"I think we should stick together," Mitch said. "We don't have any weapons. Everything is down in the hole."

"I know," Barry said. "But we stopped one zombie. We set the dogs free. And we may have done enough to finish off the other two zombies. That is, if the salt works on them, too. So we've done a lot."

Mitch nodded.

"Now we need to save Lucy and get out of here," Barry said.

"Which way?" asked Mitch.

Barry pointed to one side of the hole. "It looks easier to walk that way," he said.

But as soon as they had taken their first steps, the zombies charged at them from behind a tree! One grabbed Mitch and the other grabbed Barry.

Barry put both hands on the zombie's arm and tried to push him away. The zombie was covered in salty grime. Barry was, too.

115

The zombie knocked him to the ground. Barry swung both fists, but he could only hit the zombie's chest. He needed to hit its nose.

"Keep fighting!" Mitch called.

"Whack its nose if you can!" Barry yelled. He crawled to his knees, but the zombie held tight.

Barry managed to reach his flashlight. He swung hard and hit the zombie's nose. For a second, the zombie's grip was looser. Barry pulled free.

Barry ran several feet away. But the second zombie turned toward Mitch. Both zombies had him now! Mitch would never get free.

"Save yourself!" Mitch called. "Get away and get help."

But Barry would never leave Mitch. There was no time to get help. He ran toward the zombies and punched them in the back. Salty ooze went everywhere.

The zombies seemed to be getting weaker. But together, two weak zombies were still stronger than Mitch. Barry kept punching, but they didn't let go of Mitch.

Barry pulled on a zombie's shoulders. The other had Mitch tight in both arms. And he was leaning toward Mitch's neck. He was about to bite him!

Suddenly Barry saw a white streak coming down the hill at full speed. And he heard a familiar bark.

It was Lucy! She flung herself at the zombies, knocking them down. Mitch got loose. As the zombies staggered at the edge of the hole, Lucy leaped at one. It fell backward into the pit.

The zombie landed with a sickening thud.

Lucy wasn't done. She knocked the third zombie into the pit, too. Barry heard bones breaking as the zombie fell ten feet and crashed.

"Lucy!" Barry shouted. He hugged his dog tight. "You're a hero! We were trying to save you, but you saved us instead." Barry was crying. "Where have you been, girl? I was so scared for you."

Lucy licked his face and wagged her tail.

"You stay right by me now," Barry said. He shined his light into the pit. All three zombies were lying still on their backs. Their mouths were open. The salty gunk was dripping from every opening.

"Done?" Mitch asked.

Barry nodded. "Let's not take any chances," he said. He pointed to the two bags of salt. "Aim carefully."

The boys each picked up a bag and tore it open. They aimed the stream of salt at the zombies' mouths.

"Fill them up," Barry said. "If there's any spark left in those brains, we need to stop it."

They threw branches and leaves of top

of the zombies. "We'll fill that hole later," Barry said. "Those zombies are finished now. They won't hurt anything else."

As they turned to walk home, Barry noticed two pale white lights up ahead. They got closer, and he could see that it was Alma and her dog.

"I thought you were afraid to come this far," Barry said. "What changed your mind?"

"You needed help," Alma said. "When my Lucy came back, I felt safe again."

Barry patted his own dog. "I know what you mean," he said. "This one saved our lives."

Alma looked down. "I'm sorry I kept her from you."

"You did?"

"Yes," Alma said. "I was frightened."

"So you lied to me?" Barry said. "You had her all along?"

"Your Lucy kept me safe."

"But how did you keep her?" Barry asked. "She's not a ghost. Why couldn't she get away?"

"Lucy is a pure spirit," Alma said. "You're right, she is not a ghost. But when she's with me, she becomes pure again. She doesn't need her body. So she becomes like a ghost. Like me."

"I don't get it," Barry said. He patted Lucy again. "She's solid. She's alive."

"A pure soul like her can leave her body and come back to it," Alma said. "Your dog is very special. She can protect the living, like you. And she can protect the dead, like me."

"But she's alive, for sure," Mitch said.

"Yes," Alma agreed. "Very few souls are as pure as she is. Most are either a body or a spirit. Like us."

Barry kneeled next to Lucy. "You sure are special, girl," he said. "Let's get you home. You must be starving. I am, too."

"It takes a pure soul like her to rid the world of evil," Alma said. "If we were all as good as she, there would be no zombies to worry about."

"Well," Barry said, pointing to the pit, "at least we don't have to worry about those three anymore. But you didn't explain how you kept Lucy with you. She should have come running back to me."

Alma looked sad. "I kept her leashed," she said. "I'm sorry. But I needed her more than you did."

Chapter 17:
Back to Normal?

Barry, Mitch, and Lucy sat by the Mumford gravestone to rest for a few minutes. Alma and her dog were gone.

"I guess we'll never see them again," Barry said softly.

"We shouldn't," Mitch said. "She needs to be at rest. Her dog does, too."

Barry pulled out his notebook.

Barry's Journal: Tuesday, March 22. About 2:30 a.m.?

The salt worked, but we almost didn't live to

see it. I'll never forget how slimy and gross those zombies were. They smelled like the worst cheese and rotten fish. And they were so strong. Even as they were dying, they gripped us like we were caught in a vise. Every inch of me is covered in salt, blood, dirt, and gunk. Disgusting.

Alma is wrong. I needed Lucy more than she did. She's my dog. I love her. I am so glad to have her back. And I can tell that Lucy is glad, too.

Lucy is the hero,

A pure and loving spirit.

The zombies are lying in a hole.

I'll never go back near it.

"Time to go?" Mitch said.

"Yeah." Barry stood up. Lucy stayed very close to him. She'd been scared, too.

They walked slowly. Barry was tired and hungry. He was also filthy.

"I'm going to put all of these clothes in a plastic bag and seal it up," he said. "Then the whole thing goes in the trash. I'm not even going to try to get these clothes clean."

"Same here," Mitch said.

Lucy stopped walking and barked once. She was wagging her tail.

"What now, girl?" Barry said. "What do you see?"

Lucy was staring a gravestone near the path. One of the ghost dogs was sitting on the grave.

"He looks happy," Barry said.

They saw another ghost dog a little later. And the third one was resting on a grave at the bottom of the hill that led to the chapel. This was the smallest dog, the one that had a hard time getting out of the hole.

The ghost dog was wagging its tail.

"Happy to be home, aren't you?" Barry said. "You rest now. You did great tonight."

Lucy trotted ahead. She stopped after a few feet and looked back, waiting for Barry.

"You did great, too," Barry said. He

caught up to Lucy and patted her head. It was time to go home.

Time for things to get back to normal.

Avoiding Zombies
Tips from Barry Bannon

Step 1: Watch for signs of zombies. Piles of headless animals is a sure sign of zombies.

Step 2: Keep all senses on alert. Listen carefully, zombies make inhuman noises. They also smell like rotten meat.

Step 3: Bring your dog with you if you have one. Your pet can sense the zombies before you will see them, and it will alert you to their presence.

Step 4: Always keep a flashlight on you. The light distracts zombies and gives you the opportunity to run.

Step 5: Don't go in cemeteries at night. Zombies roam at night, and the best way to avoid being killed by a zombie is not to run into one.

Zombie Facts
from Barry Bannon

#1: Zombies are constantly hungry and mainly eat brains.

#2: Zombies only roam at night.

#3: Zombies infect anyone they bite.

#4: Zombies are killed by bashing in their brains.

#5: Salt kills zombies. Always keep a supply on hand.

#6: Zombies move slowly, but they can grab you quickly.

#7: Zombies smell like rotten meat.

#8: You can get away from a zombie by hitting it on the nose.

#9: Zombies work together to catch food.

#10: Zombies aren't very smart. With a little thought, you can easily outsmart them.

ABOUT THE ...

Author

Baron Specter is the pen name of Rich Wallace, who has written many novels for kids and teenagers. His latest books include the Kickers soccer series and the novel *Sports Camp*.

Illustrator

Setch Kneupper has years of experience thinking he saw a ghost, although Graveyard Diaries is the first series of books he's illustrated about the ordeal.